Cyclops D
Roller-S

There are more books About the Bailey School Kids!
Have you read these adventures?

Cyclops Doesn't Roller-Skate

by Debbie Dadey
and
Marcia Thornton Jones

illustrated by John Steven Gurney

A
LITTLE APPLE
PAPERBACK

SCHOLASTIC INC.
New York   Toronto   London   Auckland   Sydney

ISBN 0-590-84886-0

Text copyright © 1996 by Debra S. Dadey and Marcia Thornton Jones.
Illustrations copyright © 1996 by Scholastic Inc.
All rights reserved. Published by Scholastic Inc.
LITTLE APPLE, THE BAILEY SCHOOL KIDS, and THE ADVENTURES OF THE BAILEY SCHOOL KIDS are trademarks of Scholastic Inc.

12 11 10 9 8 7   6 5   7 8 9/9 0 1/0

Printed in the U.S.A.   40

First Scholastic printing, September 1996

Book design by Laurie Williams

To Randy and Melissa Thornton—MTJ

To my Texas critique group who helped me to see the way! Especially Pat Rynearson, Chris Coats, Diane Fuchs, Carol Gavounas, Anastasia Suen, and Helen Ketteman.—DD

Contents

Cyclops Doesn't Roller-Skate

1

Eyeballs

"Yee-haw!" Eddie screamed and jumped out of the oak tree. He landed within inches of his three friends. Howie, Liza, and Melody were standing under the old oak tree on the playground before school started.

Eddie lifted a broken twig like a sword. "*En garde,*" he yelled. Melody and Howie laughed at Eddie, but Liza looked very serious.

"It's not going to be funny when someone loses an eye," Liza told them.

Eddie jerked his baseball cap out of his hip pocket and pulled it over his red curly hair. "My grandmother says that all the time," he said, "but my eyeballs are just fine."

"You'll know for sure after today," Melody told Eddie.

"That's right," Howie said, dropping his blue Bailey School backpack onto the ground. "We're supposed to have our eyes checked."

"Checked for what? Cooties?" Eddie snickered.

"No, silly," Howie told him. "Checked to see if we need glasses."

"I'll never wear glasses," Eddie said. "Glasses are for sissies like Carey."

"No, they aren't," Howie said. "My dad wears glasses and he could beat your dad in basketball any day of the week."

Eddie held up his hand. "Don't go getting your shorts all ruffled. I guess there's nothing wrong with having to wear glasses. But there is something definitely wrong with Carey. Look."

The four kids turned to see Carey standing on the school steps. She was

3

staring at Eddie, batting her eyelashes and smiling.

"I think Carey's eyeballs are in love with Eddie." Melody giggled. "I think *all* of Carey's in love with Eddie!"

"You take that back!" Eddie screamed and started chasing Melody around the playground.

Melody was so busy giggling she didn't watch where she was going. The next thing she knew she ran smack into someone near the school doors.

"Excuse me. I didn't mean to —" Melody stopped talking and froze. She stared into a large metal eye and it stared right back at her.

2

One Eye

Melody shook her black braids and backed away from the eye. It was then she noticed the man below the metal eye. He was very tall and his shoulders were wide enough to fit two large potted plants. He had on blue pants and a heavy white knobby sweater. He was also wearing shiny black and green roller skates. Dark glasses rested on his big round nose and a mouth full of crowded teeth smiled down at her. The metal eye was actually in the middle of his forehead and the man reached up to flick a switch. The light on the eye went out.

"Oooops, I didn't realize this was on," the man said with a heavy accent. "Can't leave my eyeball on all the time. It might run out of juice."

"Your eyeball?" Melody squeaked as Howie, Liza, and Eddie came up beside her.

The man nodded. "Oh, that's just a little ophthalmologist joke."

Eddie stared at the huge man. "What in the world is an oopamologizer?" Eddie asked.

The man laughed so loud Eddie thought the man's crooked teeth might fall out. "I am an eye doctor," the man told Eddie. "I will be examining your eyes today for disease and strain."

"You're going to check my eyes?" Eddie said with disbelief.

"Certainly," the man said. "But now I must get my equipment into the school."

The man lifted two large boxes and skated toward the school.

"Maybe we should open the door for him, since his hands are full," Melody told Eddie.

"I don't think that'll be necessary,"

Eddie told her. He motioned toward the door. The eye doctor put one of the huge boxes on his head and used his free hand to pull the door open.

"Wow!" Melody said. "That guy must have a neck of steel."

"And an eye of steel," Eddie reminded her. "He's the last person I want looking at my eyes."

3

Dr. Polly

Mrs. Jeepers stood in front of her class. It was almost lunchtime and the third-graders at Bailey Elementary had been working hard all morning. Eddie looked at Mrs. Jeepers and wondered how many more math problems she was going to make them do.

There was something strange about Eddie's teacher. Everybody thought so. She had a way of flashing her green eyes and rubbing the mysterious brooch she always wore until the kids paid attention. Even Eddie. Most of the kids thought she was a vampire, but nobody wanted to find out for sure.

Mrs. Jeepers cleared her throat before talking in her strange Transylvanian accent. "Please put your pencils down.

We must take a brief rest from work today."

Melody stared at Mrs. Jeepers and Liza gasped, but Eddie grinned and smacked his pencil down on his desk. Ever since becoming their teacher, Mrs. Jeepers had kept them busy copying math problems and rewriting sentences until their pencils were nothing but stubs.

Eddie waved his hand high above his head. "Do we get an extra recess?" he asked.

A few kids clapped, but they stopped in a hurry when Mrs. Jeepers flashed her green eyes in their direction. "There will be no extra recess," she said quietly.

"We will stop working so you may have your eyes examined."

Mrs. Jeepers ignored Eddie when he groaned. Instead, she picked up a long white stick of chalk that was nearly the same color as her pale fingers. When she wrote on the board the chalk squeaked,

sending goose bumps up all the third-graders' backs.

"This is the name of the ophthalmologist," she said.

"That's who I ran into this morning," Melody said.

"Dr. Polly is here to look at your eyes," Mrs. Jeepers added. "I am sure you will all be very polite to him. After all, he is a guest in our school."

Eddie slid down in his seat and frowned. "I don't need to have my eyes examined," he mumbled. "Especially by a sissy doctor."

Howie shook his head and spoke so softly Eddie barely heard him. "Dr. Polly is no sissy. I have a feeling we'd better beware of Dr. Polly."

4

The Cave

Mrs. Jeepers led the long line of third-graders down the dim hallway of Bailey Elementary School. Eddie, Melody, Howie, and Liza stuck together near the end. The line snaked past the office and the cafeteria before Mrs. Jeepers led them into the gymnasium.

"Whoever heard of an eye doctor having an office in a gym?" Eddie grumbled. "What will he make us do? Shoot eyeballs through the basketball hoops?"

"His office isn't in the gym," Howie said. "It's back there." Howie pointed to a door off the back of the gym where Mrs. Jeepers was knocking. The door opened, but not like a normal door. This door slid open and disappeared into the wall.

14

Dr. Polly looked out from his dark office. "Who is here?" he asked. His deep accent echoed across the empty gym.

"Great," Eddie mumbled. "An eye doctor who can't see."

But then Dr. Polly reached up and tapped his head. When he did, the metal eye in the middle of his forehead winked on. Dr. Polly smiled at Mrs. Jeepers, showing his big crooked teeth.

"I've been waiting for you," Dr. Polly bellowed to Mrs. Jeepers. "Please, send in the little lambs."

One at a time the third-graders disappeared inside the dark room. When they came out they were quiet and pale. They all hurried out of the gym as if they couldn't wait to get back to work in the third-grade classroom.

"What do you think he's doing to everybody?" Melody whispered.

"He's just looking at their eyeballs," Eddie said.

Howie nodded. "It won't hurt a bit. All

we have to do is stare at a chart and read some letters and numbers."

Liza shook her head. "We won't be able to read a thing with the lights off."

"My grandma said reading in the dark is bad for my eyeballs," Eddie added. "Of course, most reading is bad for my eyeballs."

"After you read the chart, it has to be dark," Howie explained. "That way he can shine a light in our eyes to make sure everything is all right."

Finally, Melody and her friends were the only ones left. Dr. Polly stuck his massive shoulders out the door. His metal eye shone in their direction. "Next!" he yelled.

Eddie hopped up from the bench. But he slowed down when he got closer to the door. "It's as dark as a cave in there," he told Dr. Polly.

Dr. Polly smiled, showing his big crooked choppers. "Why, you are absolutely right. It reminds me of my island home near Greece."

Eddie glanced back at his friends and gulped before entering the pitch-black cave of Dr. Polly.

Several hours later the friends met under the oak tree. It was after school and the kids had in their hands the results of their eye exams. "I wonder why Dr. Polly used sheep pictures for his eye test?" Liza asked.

"Sheep are very popular," Howie said. "Carey even collects little sheep figures. She's crazy about them."

"Dr. Polly collects them, too," Melody said. "He told me he has hundreds of sheep at his home."

"Dr. Polly is crazy," Eddie blurted. "And he smells like an old goat."

Howie's face turned as white as the wool on a lamb. When he spoke his voice trembled. "This is worse than I thought," he said. "Much worse."

"What are you talking about?" Melody asked.

Howie took a shaky breath and looked each one of his friends in the eyes. "There's something you should know about our new doctor," he said. "But I'm afraid to tell you."

"Why?" Liza asked. "Is it something terrible?"

Howie nodded.

"Tell us," Melody urged.

Just as Howie opened his mouth to speak, a huge shadow fell across the four friends. Liza gulped and Melody ducked. Howie stared straight up in terror as Dr. Polly towered over the four kids.

5

Stinky Cheese

Dr. Polly smiled at the kids, showing his crooked teeth. "What a perfect place for a picnic," he said, sitting down beside them on the ground. He was so tall that even when he sat down the kids couldn't look straight into his sunglasses. They couldn't help but notice he still wore the shiny metal light on his forehead.

He shined the light inside a paper sack and pulled out a jug of milk and a hunk of cheese. "I always enjoy an afternoon snack of goat's milk and goat cheese," he explained to the kids.

"Pee-ew!" Eddie said as soon as Dr. Polly unwrapped the cheese.

"Would you like to try some?" Dr. Polly asked. "This is very popular where I come from."

Eddie backed away and shook his head.

"Where *are* you from?" Howie asked. "After all, we've never met a doctor that keeps pictures of sheep in his office."

"Or one that eats stinky cheese and milk," Eddie added.

Dr. Polly laughed so hard his shoulders shook. "This is the only kind of cheese and milk we have on my island," he said, pulling on his roller skates. Then he

stood up to leave, turning his metal eye on the kids. They squinted in its bright light.

"I would love to show you my little island," he said, only he wasn't laughing anymore. "I'm sure you would find it unforgettable." Without another word, he hobbled over to the sidewalk and skated away.

"Something about the way he said that gave me the creeps," Melody said.

"Everything about him gives me the creeps," Liza said. "From his dark office to that strange light on his head."

"I never want to go to his stupid island," Eddie said. "It's probably full of one-eyed doctors running around yelling 'Polly want a cracker'!"

Melody and Liza giggled, but Howie snapped his fingers. "That's it!" he said.

"What?" Eddie said. "Don't tell me you want a cracker, too?"

"No," Howie said, "but you're on the right track, and I have a feeling we're in trouble. Big trouble."

6

Cyclops

"Watch this," Howie said, popping a videotape into his machine. Melody, Liza, and Eddie had all followed Howie back to his house. Now they were in his family room in front of the television set.

"We should be doing our homework instead of watching TV," Liza reminded Howie.

"Who cares about homework?" Eddie said. "Where's the popcorn?"

Howie sat on the floor next to his friends. "This isn't anything to joke about. It's serious. Our homework can wait."

"My homework can wait until next year," Eddie said.

"Shhhh," Howie said. "Just watch."

The kids watched a short movie called

25

Odysseus and Polyphemus. It was all about this giant creature with big teeth called Cyclops. The Cyclops' name was Polyphemus. He was huge, with one eye in the middle of his forehead, but he wasn't very smart. Mostly the Cyclops tended his sheep and goats on an island all alone in the Mediterranean Sea.

Odysseus had the bad luck of landing his ship on the Cyclops' island. Polyphemus trapped Odysseus and his men inside his cave. Polyphemus ate cheese, goats, and sheep, but his favorite thing to eat was men. Polyphemus was all set to eat them. But Odysseus outsmarted Polyphemus by putting out the Cyclops' eye and helping his men escape.

When the movie was over, Eddie jumped up. "I'm hungry, let's eat."

"What about the movie?" Howie asked him. He tossed Eddie a bag of popcorn from the nearby kitchen counter.

"It was pretty good," Eddie admitted,

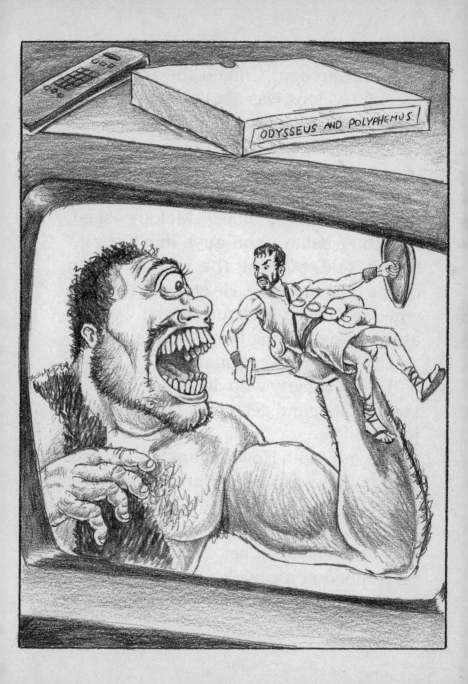

opening the bag. "I liked the part when the big Cyclops was about to put that little guy into his mouth."

"Don't you get it?" Howie asked his friends. Liza, Melody, and Eddie looked blankly at him.

"What's this all about?" Melody asked.

"I can't believe you guys don't see it," Howie said, pushing the rewind button on the tape machine. He stopped the tape when it showed a picture of the Cyclops as he was grabbing a man to eat.

"Look!" Howie commanded.

"I see a big guy who definitely needs to see a dentist and get a new hobby," Eddie joked.

"No, no, no!" Howie stamped his foot and pointed to the picture. "That's Dr. Polly. He's a Cyclops!"

Eddie laughed, spitting popcorn all over the television set. "Your head must be trapped in a cave."

"Maybe it's on that island with the Cyclops." Liza giggled.

"Stop joking," Howie squealed. "This is serious."

Melody held up her hand. "I don't think a Cyclops would come all the way to Bailey City just to check our eyes."

Liza nodded. "And a Cyclops definitely doesn't roller-skate," she told Howie.

"Howie's been watching a few too many movies," Eddie suggested. "The TV has warped his mind."

Howie folded his arms in front of him. "You can tease me all you want, but I think Dr. Polly is a Cyclops. And I'm going to prove it."

7

Bailey Kid Feast

"You can't prove Dr. Polly is a Cyclops," Melody pointed out. "Because he *isn't*."

Liza nodded. "He's just an eye doctor."

"But it all fits," Howie argued. "The sheep . . . the cave . . . and his name is Polly. As in *Polly*-phemus. He even has an eye in the middle of his forehead."

"That's not an eye," Liza told him. "It's a light. He wears it to help him see better."

"That's exactly what I've been telling you!" Howie yelled. "Without that light, he can't see a thing! It's his eyeball!"

Melody smiled and Liza tried to hide her giggle. But Eddie laughed right out loud.

"Of course he can see," Liza said.

Howie put his hands on his hips. "With what?" he asked.

"With his two eyes," Melody blurted.

"What two eyes?" Howie asked. "Have you seen them?"

"Sure we have," Eddie said, stuffing more popcorn in his mouth.

"When?" Howie asked.

Melody, Liza, and Eddie all started to speak at once. But they grew quiet when they each realized the same thing.

"Howie's right," Liza said slowly. "It's impossible to see Dr. Polly's eyes through his dark glasses and he never takes them off."

"Because he doesn't have any eyes," Howie finished, "except for that one giant eye in the middle of his forehead."

"I don't care if he has a pizza in the middle of his forehead," Eddie snapped. "We're wasting a perfectly good afternoon counting eyeballs when we could be kicking soccer balls."

"You'll care when he takes you back to

his Mediterranean cave to turn you into his Thanksgiving feast," Howie told him.

"The only Thanksgiving turkey around here is you," Eddie said.

"Not turkey," Howie said. "Kid. A Bailey kid feast."

"Dr. Polly did call us little lambs," Liza remembered. "And that movie said Cyclops monsters liked to eat goats and lambs. Baby goats are called kids. Maybe Howie's got something."

"He's got feathers for brains," Eddie said. "Dr. Polly isn't taking us anywhere. My grandmother won't even let me ride the bus to the mall. She'd never let me cruise the Mediterranean."

"Your grandmother won't be able to stop him. No one can stop him," Howie warned. "Except us!"

8

Clueless

The chilly fall wind blew dead leaves across the Bailey School playground, but Howie didn't notice. It was early the next morning and he was late meeting his friends in their favorite place. He trudged over to Melody, Liza, and Eddie. He dropped his bookbag, then plopped to the ground under the big oak tree. His three friends sat down next to him.

"What happened to you?" Liza asked. "You look like you haven't slept all night."

"I haven't," Howie mumbled. "I watched that movie over and over, hoping to get a clue."

"Hoping won't help," Eddie said.

"Don't be so sure," Howie said seriously.

"I'm sure." Eddie laughed. "Because you've been clueless for as long as I've known you."

Howie reached over and tugged Eddie's baseball cap down over his eyes. "You won't be laughing so hard when Dr. Polly snatches us from our safe little classroom."

Eddie peeked at Howie from beneath his baseball cap. "Living on a sunny island in the middle of the Mediterranean sounds much safer than spending a day in a vampire teacher's classroom."

"A Cyclops would rather eat you than look at you. But that's not all," Howie added. "I used my mom's computer to find out more about Cyclopes. Not only are they mean and eat people, but some legends say their one eye has special powers."

"What kind of power?" Liza asked.

"Like a laser beam," Howie said.

"Cool," Eddie said. "Maybe Dr. Polly

could beam Mrs. Jeepers into outer space."

"Not just Mrs. Jeepers," Howie told him. "But you, me, and all of Bailey City."

"What else did you find?" Melody asked.

Howie sighed. "Nothing. Mom had to use her computer before I could find out more."

"You really believe all this stuff, don't you?" Melody said softly.

Howie nodded so hard he bumped his head on the trunk of the giant oak tree. "And I believe we have to do something. Before it's too late."

"Do you have any ideas?" Liza asked.

"There's only one thing we can do," Howie told his friends.

Eddie grabbed a handful of leaves from the ground and tossed them in Howie's face. "The only thing we need to do is buy a rubber-lined cage for you," Eddie said with a snicker, "because

you've gone cuckoo — completely bonkers. Dr. Polly is no more a Cyclops than I am."

"I'm not sure what *you* are," Howie admitted, pulling leaves out of his hair. "But Dr. Polly is a Cyclops and I'll prove it."

9

Plan A

"My idea," Howie said with a shaky voice, "may be dangerous. Very dangerous."

"You're the dangerous one," Eddie said. "You don't even know for sure that Dr. Polly is a monster and you're plotting to throw him out of Bailey City. If you ask me, one-eyed monsters are the least of our trouble. The only thing Bailey City should beware is no-brained kids named Howie."

"What if I prove it to you?" Howie said slowly. "Then will you help me save Bailey City?"

Eddie put his hands on his hips. "If you prove it," he bragged, "I'll battle that one-eyed monster all by myself."

Melody adjusted her blue Bailey

School backpack and looked Howie in the eye. "Exactly how do you plan to prove that Dr. Polly is a one-eyed people-eating machine?"

"I'm going to snatch off his dark glasses," Howie said matter-of-factly.

"What?" Melody screeched.

Liza shook her head. "You can't just go up to a doctor and grab his glasses. For one thing, Mrs. Jeepers would zap you. Besides it'd be really rude."

"And for another thing," Melody asked, "what if Dr. Polly really *is* a Cyclops?"

"Then there won't be anything underneath his glasses," Howie told them. The four kids were quiet for a moment as they imagined Dr. Polly with no eyes, except the strange one in the middle of his forehead.

"What if he decides to blast you?" Eddie asked Howie.

"It's too dangerous," Melody told him. "You can't do it."

"I don't have any choice," Howie said. "We have to stop Dr. Polly before he makes Bailey School his next cave home."

"Bailey School isn't a cave," Liza said.

"It seems like one to me," Eddie said. "A big black cave full of monsterlike teachers and vampires and . . ."

"A Cyclops," Howie finished for Eddie.

"If you really think Dr. Polly is a Cyclops . . ." Melody said.

"I know he is," Howie said firmly.

". . . then you need to come up with a better plan," Melody told him.

"There may not be time," Liza said, pointing toward the sidewalk. "There's Dr. Polly now."

The four kids looked up to see Dr. Polly skating quickly up the sidewalk. He was smiling and the light in the middle of his forehead was shining brightly. When he was close, he stomped off the sidewalk and clomped through the grass with his skates still on. He was headed directly for them.

Howie gulped. "This is it," he whispered.

10

Safety First

"Good morning," Dr. Polly said, showing his big crooked teeth.

"H-hello," Howie said nervously. He reached his hand toward Dr. Polly's glasses.

"You know you really should wear a helmet and pads when you skate," Liza told Dr. Polly as Howie's hand crept closer to the dark glasses.

"That's right," Melody said, after grabbing Howie's hand. "If you fell you could break your neck."

"Or your eyeball," Eddie snickered.

"And that would be too bad," Howie said sarcastically.

"You are exactly right," Dr. Polly said. "I have some pads in my office, but I'll need to buy a helmet. Thanks for your

suggestion." Dr. Polly waved before stomping back over to the sidewalk. Then he glided toward the school like he was floating on a cloud.

"Why did you stop me?" Howie complained. "I could have proved he was a Cyclops."

"You could have been blasted into another time zone," Melody said.

Howie grabbed Melody's shoulder. "You mean you believe Dr. Polly is really Polyphemus?" Howie asked.

"I'm not too sure about that," Melody said. "I just don't think you should take the chance."

"There's got to be another way," Liza suggested.

"There is," Eddie told them.

"What?" Howie, Melody, and Liza said together.

Eddie stood up and brushed leaves from his jeans. "If anyone should take the risk it should be me," Eddie said.

"Why is that?" Howie asked.

"Because I'm tougher than any of you," Eddie said.

Melody jumped up and held her fist next to Eddie's nose. "You want to prove that?" she asked.

Eddie's face turned red. "No, I just thought it was the right thing to do . . . offering to help."

Liza stood up and put her hands on her hips. "Since when do you want to do the right thing?"

Eddie sat back down in a pile of leaves and threw some up in the air. "Well, excuse me for trying to help."

"You can help," Howie told him, "because now it's time for Plan B."

"Plan B?" Melody asked.

"What's that?" Eddie laughed. "Bombard him with *boogers*?"

"Very funny," Howie said. "Gather around and I'll tell you exactly what we have to do to get rid of Dr. Polly."

11

Plan B

Even though Liza whispered, her voice echoed all around the dark gym. "I don't think this is such a good idea," Liza said. "It's against school rules to be here before school. Are you sure this is the only way to save Bailey Elementary?"

Howie nodded. "According to my mom's computer, a Cyclops doesn't give up when it wants something. Dr. Polly wants to take over Bailey School. We have to stop him before he does."

"We won't be stopping anything if you keep talking," Melody warned. "He's probably around and he's bound to hear us."

Howie shook his head. "A Cyclops doesn't have good hearing, but his single eye is very strong. That's why my plan will work."

"It seems cruel," Liza said softly.

"We're being much nicer than Odysseus was," Howie pointed out. The four kids remembered how Odysseus escaped from the famous Cyclops Polyphemus by stabbing his eye with a huge wooden stake.

"That had to hurt," Eddie said.

"We're not going to hurt Dr. Polly," Howie reminded them. "Let's go."

Liza, Eddie, and Melody tiptoed behind Howie to the sliding door at the back of the gym. "Are you sure you want to do this?" Howie asked.

"It's not too late to back out," Eddie added. "We'd all understand if you're too chicken to go in there."

"I'm not chicken," Howie said. "Besides, you promised you'd go with me."

Eddie took a step back. "But that was before I remembered what happened to

some of Odysseus' men. They ended up as lunch meat!"

"So you do believe me," Howie gasped.

"We believe Dr. Polly's strange," Melody told him. "Strange enough to give us the creeps."

"So you'll help?" Howie asked.

Melody looked at Liza and Liza looked at Eddie. Then they all looked at Howie.

"We'll help you," Melody finally said.

Eddie nodded. "Go ahead. Open the door."

Howie's hands shook as he slowly rolled the wooden door open. It was so dark inside Dr. Polly's office that Howie could barely see his hand in front of his nose.

"We'll never find what we're looking for," Eddie moaned. "It's too dark."

"Of course, it's dark," Howie said. "Caves are always dark."

Just then, light flooded the tiny room.

Liza whimpered and Melody ducked. But Eddie laughed and pointed to the light switch he had just turned on. "You look like you saw a monster."

"We did," Melody snapped. "And the monster is *you!*"

"Stop," Howie told them. "We have to hurry before Dr. Polly finds us."

"Where should we look?" Melody asked.

The four friends turned in circles, looking around the tiny office.

"They have to be there," Howie finally said. He pointed to a drawer underneath the lamb eye chart. Slowly Howie pulled on the handle and the drawer opened with a loud squeak. There, neatly piled in a box, was just what they were looking for. Ten tiny lightbulbs.

"Quick, I hear something," Liza said. "Grab them and let's go."

Howie shoved the box into the bottom

of his bookbag and looked at his friends. "Without these," he said, "Dr. Polly's eyeball will be useless."

"I hope you're right," Melody said.

12

Out of Juice

It was hard to concentrate on math. Every time Howie copied down a multiplication problem, he thought about the little box of lightbulbs hidden in his bookbag. He chewed on the end of his eraser and glanced at the clock. It was almost time for recess.

When a hand gently squeezed Howie's shoulder, he jumped and his pencil hit Eddie in the back. Howie looked at the hand and saw five pointy green-painted fingernails. Mrs. Jeepers patted him on the shoulder.

"You are not looking well this morning," Mrs. Jeepers said. "Are you ill?"

Howie shook his head. "I didn't sleep well last night," he said truthfully.

Mrs. Jeepers smiled her odd little half

smile and gently rubbed the green brooch she always wore. "Perhaps some fresh air will make you feel better," she said.

"Please put your pencils down," she told the class. "We shall go outside to enjoy this lovely fall day."

Most of the kids cheered, but Howie was too worried. He headed for the oak tree as soon as he got outside. His three friends joined him.

"Do you think our plan is working?" Melody asked.

"We're about to find out," Howie said. He pointed to the sidewalk where Dr. Polly was skating.

"What is he doing?" Liza gasped. "He looks like he never skated before."

It was true. One of Dr. Polly's feet zigged, while the other foot zagged. His hands waved in crazy circles while he tried to get his balance. That's when he accidentally grabbed a second-grader's jump rope.

Eddie laughed. "He looks like a big kitten tangled in a ball of yarn."

But Dr. Polly didn't stay tangled for long. Once he was loose, he started across the playground. The kids stared at the light in the middle of Dr. Polly's head. It was definitely not as bright as yesterday. When Dr. Polly's skate hit a bump, the light flickered.

"His eyeball is almost out of juice," Howie whispered.

"Doesn't he know you can't skate on grass?" Melody asked. Dr. Polly skated faster and faster. He headed straight toward them.

"He's going to hit us!" Liza shrieked.

The four friends scattered in all directions just before Dr. Polly ran smack dab into the oak tree. *BOOM!*

"Are you okay?" Melody asked.

"Did you get hurt?" Howie said, helping Dr. Polly up from the ground.

"Just a scrape here and there," the

giant doctor said. "That tree caught me by surprise."

"You'd see better if you took off those glasses," Eddie told him. "Then you could watch where you're going."

Dr. Polly's light flickered. He tapped it and mumbled, "It must be these new knee and elbow pads. I'm not used to wearing them."

Dr. Polly pushed away from the tree and skated toward the doors of Bailey Elementary. He almost made it. Unfortunately, Dr. Polly didn't see Mrs. Jeepers!

13

Rules, Rules, Rules!

"Dr. Polly was lucky," Melody said. "Mrs. Jeepers could have made bat bait out of him."

Eddie sighed. "Maybe we should have left him alone. If his eye was juiced up, he might have zapped Mrs. Jeepers to Milwaukee."

It was after school and Howie, Liza, Melody, and Eddie were sitting in the Burger Doodle restaurant sipping thick Doodlegum Shakes.

"We were lucky that nobody got hurt," Liza said. "After all, it was partly our fault."

"Liza's right," Howie said. "We hid Dr. Polly's eyeballs . . . "

"You mean lightbulbs," Eddie said.

Howie shrugged. "Whatever they are, he couldn't see where he was going." Howie shivered when he remembered his teacher being knocked to the ground by Dr. Polly at recess. "I thought Mrs. Jeepers was going to zap us all to Ruby Mountain. Somebody should warn Dr. Polly to never mess with vampire teachers."

"I think he learned his lesson," Melody said. "And that's why Principal Davis announced Dr. Polly was finished checking everyone's eyes. He packed up and left."

"That's not all Principal Davis said," Eddie griped. "Now everybody has to wear helmets and knee pads to skate. Rules, rules, rules. I'm sick of Bailey School rules."

"It's for our own safety," Howie told Eddie as he stirred his thick vanilla shake.

"That's what you said about grabbing

Dr. Polly's lightbulbs," Eddie said. "But Dr. Polly is no Cyclops. He's just a bad skater with cheap sunglasses."

"What makes you so sure?" Melody asked.

"Because," Eddie said, nodding toward the window, "there he is. And he's following Principal Davis's new rule. He's wearing a helmet that goes all the way down to his eyebrows. If he were a real Cyclops, he wouldn't be able to see a thing."

Howie, Melody, and Liza crowded around the Burger Doodle window just in time to see Dr. Polly skate across the street.

"I guess we were silly to think he was a one-eyed monster," Liza said.

Melody giggled. "After all, a Cyclops doesn't roller-skate."

"I guess you're right," Howie said, staring at Dr. Polly as he skated past them. Then Howie gasped and Melody nearly

choked. Eddie was so surprised, he spit milkshake all over the window.

There, in the middle of Dr. Polly's helmet, was a bright light that looked exactly like a giant eyeball!

Debbie Dadey and Marcia Thornton Jones have fun writing stories together. When they both worked at an elementary school in Lexington, Kentucky, Debbie was the school librarian and Marcia was a teacher. During their lunch break in the school cafeteria, they came up with the idea of the Bailey School kids.

Recently Debbie and her family moved to Aurora, Illinois. Marcia and her husband still live in Kentucky where she continues to teach. How do these authors still write together? They talk on the phone and use computers and fax machines!

The Adventures of
THE BAILEY SCHOOL KIDS™

Frankenstein Doesn't Plant Petunias, Ghosts Don't Eat Potato Chips, and Aliens Don't Wear Braces ... or do they?

Find out about the creepiest, weirdest, funniest things that happen to The Bailey School Kids!™ Collect and read them all!

❑ BAS43411-X	Vampires Don't Wear Polka Dots	$2.99
❑ BAS44061-6	Werewolves Don't Go to Summer Camp	$2.99
❑ BAS44477-8	Santa Claus Doesn't Mop Floors	$2.99
❑ BAS44822-6	Leprechauns Don't Play Basketball	$2.99
❑ BAS45854-X	Ghosts Don't Eat Potato Chips	$2.99
❑ BAS47071-X	Frankenstein Doesn't Plant Petunias	$2.99
❑ BAS47070-1	Aliens Don't Wear Braces	$2.99
❑ BAS47297-6	Genies Don't Ride Bicycles	$2.99
❑ BAS47298-4	Pirates Don't Wear Pink Sunglasses	$2.99
❑ BAS48112-6	Witches Don't Do Backflips	$2.99
❑ BAS48113-4	Skeletons Don't Play Tubas	$2.99
❑ BAS48114-2	Cupid Doesn't Flip Hamburgers	$2.99
❑ BAS48115-0	Gremlins Don't Chew Bubble Gum	$2.99
❑ BAS22635-5	Monsters Don't Scuba Dive	$2.99
❑ BAS22636-3	Zombies Don't Play Soccer	$2.99
❑ BAS22638-X	Dracula Doesn't Drink Lemonade	$2.99
❑ BAS22637-1	Elves Don't Wear Hard Hats	$2.99
❑ BAS50960-8	Martians Don't Take Temperatures	$2.99
❑ BAS50961-6	Gargoyles Don't Drive School Buses	$2.99
❑ BAS50962-4	Wizards Don't Need Computers	$2.99
❑ BAS22639-8	Mummies Don't Coach Softball	$2.99
❑ BAS84886-0	Cyclops Doesn't Roller-Skate	$2.99
❑ BAS88134-5	Bailey School Kids Super Special #1 Mrs. Jeepers Is Missing!	$4.99

Available wherever you buy books, or use this order form

Scholastic Inc., P.O. Box 7502, 2931 East McCarty Street, Jefferson City, MO 65102

Please send me the books I have checked above. I am enclosing $_____ (please add $2.00 to cover shipping and handling). Send check or money order — no cash or C.O.D.s please.

Name _____

Address _____

City_____ State/Zip _____

Please allow four to six weeks for delivery. Offer good in the U.S. only. Sorry, mail orders are not available to residents of Canada. Prices subject to change.   BSK396

Amber Brown is ready for the fourth grade.
Is the fourth grade ready for Amber Brown?

AMBER BROWN

GOES FOURTH

BY PAULA DANZIGER

Amber is all set for
a new school year.
She has new sneakers,
new notebooks —
new everything.
Now all Amber needs
is a new best friend!

Coming in October to bookstores everywhere.

Don't miss Amber's other adventures:
AMBER BROWN IS NOT A CRAYON
YOUR CAN'T EAT YOUR CHICKEN POX, AMBER BROWN

AB396

THE LEFTOVERS

by Tristan Howard

Don't be left out!

The Leftovers are the wackiest team in any league.
No matter what the sport, fun and laughs are always
part of the game plan.

BASEBALL:

❑ BBS56923-6　**The Leftovers #1: Strike Out!**　　$2.99

❑ BBS56924-4　**The Leftovers #2: Catch Flies!**　　$2.99

SOCCER:

❑ BBS89896-5　**The Leftovers #3: Use Their Heads!**　$2.99

❑ BBS92133-9　**The Leftovers #4: Reach Their Goal!**　$2.99

Available wherever you buy books or use this order form.
